A Mango
in the Hand
A Story Told Through Proverbs

by Antonio Sacre

Illustrated by Sebastià Serra

Abrams Books for Young Readers
New York

About this book:

Proverbs, called the shortest
art form, teach us a life lesson.
Similar ones exist in many cultures.

The illustrations
in this book were created
using pencil and ink on parchment paper and
then digitally colored.

Library of Congress Cataloging-in-Publication Data

Sacre, Antonio, 1968–
A mango in the hand : a story told through proverbs / Antonio Sacre ;
illustrated by Sebastià Serra.
p. cm.
Summary: Guided by proverbs from his father and other relatives, Francisco makes
several attempts to bring ripe mangos home for dessert on his saint day, and in the process
learns lessons in love and generosity. Includes glossary of Spanish terms.
ISBN 978-0-8109-9734-9 (alk. paper)
[1. Family life—Cuba—Fiction. 2. Conduct of life—Fiction. 3. Mango—Fiction. 4. Proverbs—
Fiction. 5. Cuba—Fiction.] I. Serra, Sebastià, 1966– ill. II. Title.
PZ7.S1226Man 2011
[E]—dc22
2010024423

Text copyright © 2011 Antonio Sacre
Illustrations copyright © 2011 Sebastià Serra
Book design by Melissa Arnst

Printed and bound in China
15 14 13 12 11 10 9 8 7 6

Abrams Books for Young Readers are available at special discounts when purchased in quantity
for premiums and promotions as well as fundraising or educational use. Special editions
can also be created to specification. For details, contact specialsales@abramsbooks.com
or the address below.

ABRAMS The Art of Books
195 Broadway, New York, NY 10007
abramsbooks.com

To Talia Jacq Paley
—A. S.

To Ramon, Susanna, Èlia, Eduard, and Marcel,
whose open hearts and open hands offer smiles
(and sometimes sweet mangos) everywhere they go
—S. S.

Francisco woke to the smell of *café con leche* and the sound of his father's laughter.

"Are you going to sleep all day?" his father asked. "*¡Camarón que se duerme, se lo lleva la corriente!* If the little shrimp sleeps all day, the current will take him away! It's finally here, *el día de San Francisco,* your saint day. *¡Toma!* Drink!" Papá handed Francisco a glass of strong coffee loaded with sweet milk and sugar, warmed just right.

Francisco wiped his eyes, took the glass in his hands, and carefully took a sip. One of his eyes popped open! He took another sip, and his other eye popped open!

"Mamá and I are making *ropa vieja, tostones, y aguacate* for your feast day. What do you want for dessert?" Papá asked.

"Some delicious mangos, right from the tree!"

Tostones

Aguacate

Ropa vieja

"I think you are old enough to get the mangos," said Papá.

"All by myself?"

"Yes, *mi'jo.*"

"*¡Qué padre!*"

"Do you remember where the tree is?" asked Papá.

"*Sí*, Papá. Past Tío Tito's house, and Abuela's house, and crabby Tía Clara's house, through the park, to the mango tree."

"Very good! You remember! And Tía Clara is not crabby. She is just lonely. Go bring us back some mangos!" said Papá.

Francisco walked a long way, longer than he had ever walked by himself. He walked past Tío Tito's house. Tío Tito waved. Francisco waved back.

He walked past Abuela's house, and she waved. He waved back. He walked past crabby Tía Clara's house. He thought he saw her looking out from behind the curtain, but when he waved, the curtain quickly closed.

Francisco walked through the park, past the boys and girls playing *pelota*, and finally found the mango tree, full of many ripe, juicy mangos.

When he reached toward a branch, a bee buzzed loudly in his ear. Yikes! The tree buzzed with bees! Everywhere he looked, he saw a bee!

He ran—past the *pelota* game, past crabby Tía Clara's house, past Abuela's house, past Tío Tito's house, and back to his home.

Papá asked, "Did you find the mango tree?"

Francisco said, "Yes, it had a hundred mangos on it!"

"Wow! How many did you bring home?"

"Well, none," Francisco said.

"*Ay, niño, mejor un mango en la mano que cien en el árbol.* Better one mango in the hand than a hundred in the tree. What happened?"

Francisco looked at Papá, but didn't say anything.

"*La verdad, por dura que sea.* The truth, no matter how hard it is," Papá said in an encouraging tone.

"I was scared of the bees," said Francisco.

"Bees?" asked Papá.

"There were billions!" replied Francisco.

Papá raised an eyebrow.

"Or maybe millions!"

Papá raised the other eyebrow.

"At least a thousand!"

Papá crossed his arms, lowered his eyebrows, and asked, "How many bees were there *really*?"

"A lot! At least ten. Or twelve!"

Papá laughed, hugged his son, and said, "*Mi'jo, no hay mal que por bien no venga.* Nothing bad happens that good doesn't come of it. Don't be scared of the bees! Without them, the mangos would not be as sweet. Take my hat and gently shoo the bees away. Don't swat at them—they will get mad. Just shoo them away, and bring us back some mangos!"

Francisco walked
past Tío Tito's house,

past Abuela's house, and past
crabby Tía Clara's house.

They all waved, except for crabby Tía Clara, who stood on her porch alone.

At the mango tree, Francisco gently shooed the bees away with Papá's hat. He climbed onto a branch and filled the hat with so many red, ripe, juicy mangos that he had to hold on to the hat with both hands!

Francisco balanced the hat between his stomach and the trunk, and scooted down the tree. But this caused all the mangos to be smashed and smushed, making a gooey mess on his shirt and in the hat. When the bees smelled the sweet mango juice, they buzzed excitedly and swarmed toward the boy. Francisco threw down the hat, ripped off his shirt, and ran back home.

Crabby Tía Clara saw a streaking, half-naked little boy, and she yelled, in a quite crabby way, "Put on some clothes!"

Abuela looked up from her mower and cried, "He's naked!"

Tío Tito shouted, "That's my boy!"

When Francisco arrived home, Papá was waiting at the front door with a towel. He threw it around his son and sat down next to him.

"*Mi'jo*, I sent you out the door with one shirt and one hat to pick mangos, and you come back with no shirt, no hat, and no mangos! What happened?"

Francisco told him. Papá laughed and said, "*Él que mucho abarca, poco aprieta.* He who tries to grab too much, gets little. So that is why crabby—I mean, lonely—Tía Clara called me, and Abuela, and Tío Tito. News travels fast in this neighborhood! Let's clean you up. *Él que temprano se moja, tiempo tiene de secarse.* He who gets drenched at dawn has all day to dry off."

"Can you come with me, Papá?"

"You can do it by yourself, *mi'jo. Querer es poder.* Where there's a will, there's a way."

Francisco had a will—there had to be a way.

Dressed in a new shirt, Francisco walked past Tío Tito's, Abuela's, and Tía Clara's houses, and walked right to the tree.

He climbed it and picked one mango. He put the mango under his chin, climbed down, and placed it in his father's hat. He did it again, and again, and again. Soon he had a lot of red, ripe, juicy mangos! He gathered up Papá's hat and started home. When he got to crabby Tía Clara's house, he stopped. Although laughter could be heard from Tío Tito's and Abuela's homes, no sound came from Tía Clara's house.

Franscisco slowly walked up her long, long walkway and hesitantly knocked on her door.

"What do you want?" she asked, looking crabbier than ever.

"I thought maybe you'd like some company—and a mango." Franscisco offered her the fruit.

"It probably has bees swarming around it!"

"Tía, there aren't any bees, and besides, *no hay mal que por bien no venga.* The bees make the fruit sweet!"

"Where did you learn that?" she asked, her face softening just the tiniest bit.

"From my dad," Francisco said.

"I used to say that to him when he was your age," she said. "I also told him, *dime con quien andas, y te digo quien eres.*"

"What does that mean?" he asked.

"Tell me with whom you walk, and I'll tell you who you are."

Francisco again held the mango out to her. "Would you like one of my mangos?"

"You worked hard for that mango," she said, and didn't sound so crabby after all.

"I have plenty. This one is for you." He gave her the fruit. She turned around, went indoors, and gently closed the door.

Francisco walked to Abuela's house.

"¡Abuela! ¿Quieres mangos?"

"*Gracias, mi'jito, ¡pero pan para hoy, hambre para mañana!* Thanks, but if you eat all your bread today, you'll be hungry tomorrow!" He gave her a mango anyway. She smiled.

When he walked to Tío Tito's house, Tío Tito and his friends were playing dominos.

"Hey, you've got mangos!" All the men shouted, "*¡Qué bien!*"

Tío Tito said, "Way to go! I'll show you how to make an *oso*, a bear, out of a mango." He pulled out a pocketknife from his *guayabera*, took a mango from the hat, and cut and peeled and cut and peeled, and there it was, a fierce bear from the mango!

"Wow!" said Francisco.

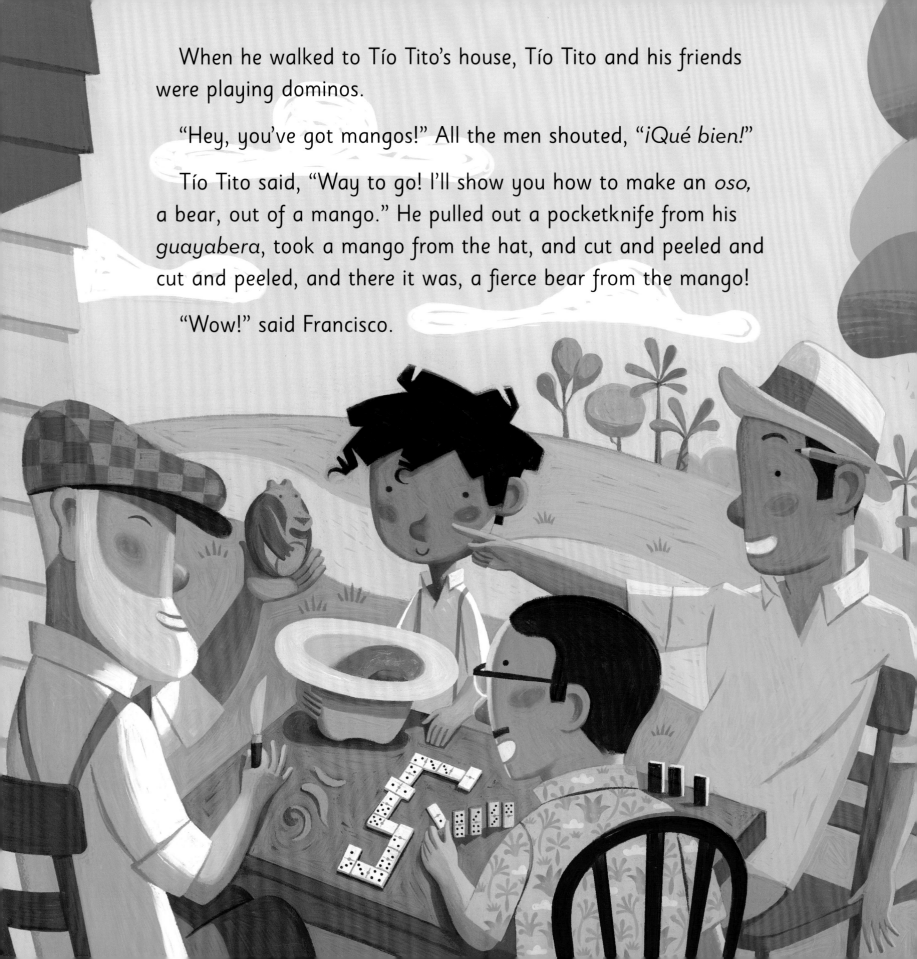

One of the other men said,
"And I can make a *toro*." He took
the knife and cut and peeled and cut and peeled,
and there it was, a charging bull in the mango!

Another said, "And I can make a *león,* a
roaring lion!"

He cut and peeled and cut and peeled, and
there it was, a roaring lion in the mango!

"*¡Adiós,* Tío!"

"*¡Adiós,* Francisco!"

He ran home, and the
men ate their mango
animals. Delicious!

"Did you get the mangos?" asked Papá.

"I did!"

"Where are they?"

Francisco looked into Papá's hat. It was empty! He turned it upside down. Still empty! He turned it over and over. Still empty!

"I gave them all away!"

"Well, *mi'jo*, it looks like you learned a valuable lesson."

"What's that?"

"*Es mejor dar que recibir.* Sometimes, it's better to give than to receive."

So Papá, Mamá, and Francisco sat down to eat Francisco's feast day meal. While they were eating, the doorbell rang. Tío Tito and his friends poured inside the house. Abuela walked in behind them with fresh cut roses.

"*¡Mangos para hoy, pan para mañana!* Mangos today, bread tomorrow! I ate my mango as soon as you gave it to me, it was so sweet," Abuela said.

"We ate ours, too!" said the men.

The door rang again. Guess who walked in?

Crabby Tía Clara—but she was not crabby at all! And she was holding a big hat full of ripe, red, juicy mangos.

She smiled and said, "I did what you did, Francisco. I shooed the bees away and got all of these mangos. Then I thought, *amor con amor se paga. Love is repaid with love.*"

Then everyone sat down and ate the gift of mangos. And Tía Clara smiled the sweetest smile ever and said, "*Barriga llena, corazón contento.* Full stomach, happy heart."

Hacerín, hacerado, este cuento se ha acabado. The end.

Glossary of Spanish
words and phrases

Abuela: grandmother

"¡Abuela! ¿Quieres mangos?": "Grandma! Do you want some mangos?"

aguacate: avocado

café con leche: a drink given to young children, made of mostly sugar, hot milk, and a touch of strong coffee

el día de San Francisco: the feast of the saint that Francisco was named after, a day more celebrated than one's own birthday for many people

guayabera: a typical shirt with four pockets in the front; it can be fancy or plain, and is considered dressy

Hacerín, hacerado, este cuento se ha acabado: a rhyme that doesn't really translate. It is a typical Cuban way to say, "The end."

mi'jo or mi'jito: contractions of *mi hijo,* a term of endearment that means "my son" or "my boy"

Paco or Paquito (little Paco): nicknames for the name Francisco

pelota: ball (in this case, baseball)

"¡Qué bien!": "How great!"

"¡Qué padre!": a pun that I borrow from my Mexican friends. *Padre* means "father," but used this way, it means "Cool!"

ropa vieja: literally, "old clothes"; also the name of a dish consisting of shredded beef in tomato sauce

Tía: aunt

Tío: uncle

tostones: fried plantains (plantains are a fruit similar to bananas)